PIGLET IS ENTIRELY SURROUNDED BY WATER

PIGLET IS ENTIRELY SURROUNDED BY WATER

A.A. MILNE

illustrated by
ERNEST H. SHEPARD

TED SMART

PIGLET IS ENTIRELY SURROUNDED BY WATER

It rained and it rained and it rained.
Piglet told himself that never in all
his life, and *he* was goodness knows *how*
old – three, was it, or four? – never
had he seen so much rain. Days and days
and days.

'If only,' he thought, as he looked
out of the window, 'I had been in Pooh's

house, or Christopher Robin's house, or
Rabbit's house when it began to rain, then
I should have had Company all this time,
instead of being here all alone, with
nothing to do except wonder when it will
stop.' And he imagined himself with
Pooh, saying, 'Did you ever see such rain,
Pooh?' and Pooh saying, 'Isn't it *awful*,
Piglet?' and Piglet saying, 'I wonder
how it is over Christopher Robin's way,'
and Pooh saying, 'I should think poor
old Rabbit is about flooded out by this
time.' It would have been jolly to talk
like this, and really, it wasn't much good
having anything exciting like floods, if
you couldn't share them with somebody.

For it was rather exciting. The
little dry ditches in which Piglet had
nosed about so often had become streams,
the little streams across which he had
splashed were rivers, and the river,
between whose steep banks they had played

so happily, had sprawled out of its own bed and was taking up so much room everywhere, that Piglet was beginning to wonder whether it would be coming into *his* bed soon.

'It's a little Anxious,' he said to himself, 'to be a Very Small Animal Entirely Surrounded by Water. Christopher Robin and Pooh could escape by Climbing Trees, and Kanga could escape by Jumping, and Rabbit could escape by Burrowing, and Owl could escape by Flying, and Eeyore could escape by – by Making a Loud Noise Until Rescued, and here am I, surrounded by water and I can't do *anything*.'

It went on raining, and every day the water got a little higher, until now it was nearly up to Piglet's window . . . and still he hadn't done anything.

'There's Pooh,' he thought to himself. 'Pooh hasn't much Brain, but he never comes to any harm. He does silly things

and they turn out right. There's Owl.
Owl hasn't exactly got Brain, but he
Knows Things. He would know the
Right Thing to do when Surrounded
by Water. There's
Rabbit. He hasn't
Learnt in Books,
but he can always
Think of a Clever
Plan. There's Kanga.
She isn't Clever, Kanga
isn't, but she would
be so anxious
about Roo that she
would do a Good Thing to do without
thinking about it. And then there's Eeyore.
And Eeyore is so miserable anyhow that he
wouldn't mind about this. But I wonder
what Christopher Robin would do?'

Then suddenly he remembered
a story which Christopher Robin
had told him about a man on a

desert island who had written something
in a bottle and thrown it into the sea;
and Piglet thought that if he wrote something
in a bottle and threw it in the water,
perhaps somebody would come and rescue *him*!

He left the window and began to search
his house, all of it that wasn't under
water, and at last he found a pencil and
a small piece of dry paper, and a bottle
with a cork to it. And he wrote on one
side of the paper:

HELP!
PIGLIT (ME)

and on the other side:

IT'S ME PIGLIT, HELP HELP!

Then he put the paper in the bottle,
and he corked the bottle up as tightly as
he could, and leant out of his window as
far as he could lean without falling in,
and he threw the bottle as far as he could

throw – *splash!* – and in a little while it
bobbed up again on the water; and he
watched it floating slowly away in the distance,
until his eyes ached with looking,

and sometimes he thought it was the bottle,
and sometimes he thought it was just a ripple
on the water which he was following, and
then suddenly he knew that he would never
see it again and that he had done all that
he could do to save himself.

'So now,' he thought, 'somebody else
will have to do something, and I hope they
will do it soon, because if they don't I
shall have to swim, which I can't, so I
hope they do it soon.' And then he gave a

very long sigh and said, 'I wish Pooh were
here. It's so much more friendly
with two.'

When the rain began Pooh was asleep.
It rained, and it rained, and it rained,
and he slept and he slept and he slept.
He had had a tiring day. You remember how
he discovered the North Pole; well, he
was so proud of this that he asked Christopher
Robin if there were any other Poles such as
a Bear of Little Brain might discover.

'There's a South Pole,' said Christopher
Robin, 'and I expect there's an East
Pole and a West Pole, though people

don't like talking about them.'

Pooh was very excited when he heard
this, and suggested that they should have
an Expotition to discover the East Pole, but
Christopher Robin had thought of something
else to do with Kanga; so Pooh went
out to discover the East Pole by himself.
Whether he discovered it or not, I forget;
but he was so tired when he got home that,
in the very middle of his supper, after he
had been eating for little more than
half-an-hour, he fell fast asleep in his chair,
and slept and slept and slept.

Then suddenly he was dreaming. He was
at the East Pole, and it was a very cold
pole with the coldest sort of snow and
ice all over it. He had found a beehive
to sleep in, but there wasn't room for his
legs, so he had left them outside. And
Wild Woozles, such as inhabit the East Pole,
came and nibbled all the fur off his legs
to make Nests for their Young. And the

more they nibbled, the colder his legs
got, until suddenly he woke up with an
Ow! – and there his was, sitting in his
chair with his feet in the water, and
water all round him!

He splashed to his door and looked out…
'This is Serious,' said Pooh. 'I must
have an Escape'

So he took his largest pot of honey
and escaped with it to a broad branch of
his tree, well above the water, and then
he climbed down again and escaped with
another pot…and when the whole Escape
was finished, there was Pooh sitting on
his branch, dangling his legs, and there,
beside him, were ten pots of honey…

Two days later, there was Pooh, sitting
on his branch, dangling his legs, and
there, beside him, were four pots of
honey…

Three days later, there was Pooh, sitting
on his branch, dangling his legs, and there
beside him, was one pot of honey.

Four days later, there was Pooh…

And it was on the morning of the fourth
day that Piglet's bottle came floating past
him, and with one loud cry of 'Honey!'
Pooh plunged into the water, seized the
bottle, and struggled back to his tree again.

'Bother!' said Pooh, as he opened it.
'All that wet for nothing. What's that bit
of paper doing?'

He took it out and looked at it.

'It's a Missage,' he said to himself,

'that's what it is. And that letter is a "P", and so is that, and so is that, and "P" means "Pooh", so it's a very important Missage to me, and I can't read it. I must find Christopher Robin or Owl or Piglet, one of those Clever Readers who can read things, and they will tell me what this missage means. Only I can't swim. Bother!'

Then he had an idea, and I think that for a Bear of Very Little Brain, it was a good idea. He said to himself:

'If a bottle can float, then a jar can float, and if a jar floats, I can sit on the top of it, if it's a very big jar.'

So he took his biggest jar, and corked it up.

'All boats have to have a name,' he said, 'so I shall call mine *The Floating Bear*.' And with these words he dropped his boat into the water and jumped in after it.

For a little while Pooh and *The Floating Bear*
were uncertain as to which of them
was meant to be on the top, but after trying

one or two different positions, they settled
down with *The Floating Bear* underneath
and Pooh triumphantly astride it, paddling
vigorously with his feet.

Christopher Robin lived at the very
top of the Forest. It rained, and it rained,

and it rained, but the water
couldn't come up to *his* house. It was
rather jolly to look down into the valleys
and see the water all round him, but it
rained so hard that he stayed indoors most
of the time, and thought about things.
Every morning he went out with his umbrella
and put a stick in the place where the
water came up to, and every next morning
he went out and couldn't see his stick
any more, so he put another stick in the
place where the water came up to, and then
he walked home again, and each morning he

had a shorter walk to walk than he had had the morning before. On the morning of the fifth day he saw the water all round him, and knew that for the first time in his life he was on a real island. Which was very exciting.

It was on this morning that Owl came flying over the water to say 'How do you do?' to his friend Christopher Robin.

'I say, Owl,' said Christopher Robin, 'isn't this fun? I'm on an island!'

'The atmospheric conditions have been very unfavourable lately,' said Owl.

'The what?'

'It has been raining,' explained Owl.

'Yes,' said Christopher Robin. 'It has.'

'The flood-level has reached an unprecedented height.'

'The who?'

'There's a lot of water about,' explained Owl.

'Yes,' said Christopher Robin,
'there is.'

'However, the prospects are rapidly
becoming more favourable. At any moment—'

'Have you seen Pooh?'

'No. At any moment—'

'I hope he's all right,' said Christopher Robin. 'I've been wondering about him. I expect Piglet's with him. Do you think they're all right, Owl?'

'I expect so. You see, at any moment—'

'Do go and see, Owl. Because Pooh hasn't got very much brain, and he might do something silly, and I do love him so, Owl. Do you see, Owl?'

'That's all right,' said Owl. 'I'll go. Back directly.' And he flew off.

In a little while he was back again.

'Pooh isn't there,' he said.

'Not there?'

'He's *been* there. He's been sitting on a branch of his tree outside his house with nine pots of honey. But he isn't there now.'

'Oh, Pooh!' cried Christopher Robin. 'Where *are* you?'

'Here I am,' said a growly voice behind him.

'Pooh!'

They rushed into each other's arms.

'How did you get here, Pooh?' asked Christopher Robin, when he was ready to talk again.

'On my boat,' said Pooh proudly. 'I had a Very Important Missage sent me in a bottle, and owing to having got some water in my eyes, I couldn't read it, so I brought it to you. On my boat.'

With these proud words he gave Christopher Robin the message.

'But it's from Piglet!' cried Christopher Robin when he had read it.

'Isn't there anything about Pooh in it?' asked Bear, looking over his shoulder.

Christopher Robin read the message aloud.

'Oh, are those "P's" piglets? I thought they were poohs.'

'We must rescue him at once! I thought he was with *you*, Pooh. Owl, could you rescue him on your back?'

'I don't think so,' said Owl, after grave thought. 'It is doubtful if the necessary dorsal muscles—'

'Then would you fly to him at *once* and say that Rescue is Coming? And Pooh and I will think of a Rescue and come as quick as ever we can. Oh, don't *talk*, Owl, go on quick!' And, still thinking of something to say, Owl flew off.

'Now then, Pooh,' said Christopher Robin, 'where's your boat?'

'I ought to say,' explained Pooh as they walked down to the shore of the

island, 'that it isn't just an ordinary
sort of boat. Sometimes it's a Boat,
and sometimes it's more of an Accident.
It all depends.'

'Depends on what?'

'On whether I'm on the top of it or
underneath it.'

'Oh! Well, where is it?'

'There!' said Pooh, pointing proudly to
The Floating Bear.

It wasn't what Christopher Robin
expected, and the more he looked at it, the
more he thought what a Brave and Clever

Bear Pooh was, and the more Christopher
Robin thought this, the more Pooh looked
modestly down his nose and tried to pretend
he wasn't.

'But it's too small for two of us,' said
Christopher Robin sadly.

'Three of us with Piglet.'

'That makes it smaller still. Oh,
Pooh Bear, what shall we do?'

And then this Bear, Pooh Bear, Winnie-
the-Pooh, F.O.P. (Friend of Piglet's), R.C.
(Rabbit's Companion), P.D. (Pole Discoverer),
E.C. and T.F. (Eeyore's Comforter and Tail-
Finder) – in fact, Pooh himself – said
something so clever that Christopher Robin
could only look at him with mouth open
and eyes staring, wondering if this was
really the Bear of Very Little Brain
whom he had known and loved so long.

'We might go in your umbrella,'
said Pooh.

'?'

'We might go in your umbrella,'
said Pooh.

'??'

'We might go in your umbrella,'
said Pooh.

'!!!!!!'

For suddenly Christopher Robin saw that they
might. He opened his umbrella and put it point
downwards in the water. It floated but
wobbled. Pooh got in. He was just beginning to
say that it was all right now, when he found that it

wasn't, so after a short drink, which he didn't really want, he waded back to Christopher Robin. Then they both got in together, and it wobbled no longer.

'I shall call this boat *The Brain of Pooh*,' said Christopher Robin, and *The Brain of Pooh* set sail forthwith in a south-westerly direction, revolving gracefully.

You can imagine Piglet's joy when at last the ship came in sight of him. In after-years he liked to think that he had been in Very Great Danger during the Terrible Flood, but the only danger he had really been in was the last half-hour of his imprisonment, when Owl, who had just flown up, sat on a branch of his tree to comfort him, and told him a very long story about an aunt who had once laid a seagull's egg by mistake, and the story went on and on, rather like this sentence, until Piglet who was listening out of his

window without much hope, went to sleep
quietly and naturally, slipping slowly
out of the window towards the water
until he was only hanging on by his toes,
at which moment, luckily, a sudden loud
squawk from Owl, which was really part
of the story, being what his aunt said,
woke the Piglet up and just gave him time

to jerk himself back into safety and say, 'How interesting, and did she?' when – well, you can imagine his joy when at last he saw the good ship, *Brain of Pooh* (*Captain*, C. Robin: *1st Mate*, P. Bear) coming over the sea to rescue him. . . .

And as that is really the end of the story, and I am very tired after that last sentence, I think I shall stop there.

Piglet is Entirely Surrounded by Water
is taken from *Winnie-the-Pooh*
originally published in Great Britain 14th October 1926
by Methuen & Co. Ltd.
Text by A.A.Milne and line drawings by Ernest H.Shepard
copyright under the Berne Convention

First published 1990 by Methuen Children's Books
an imprint of Egmont Children's Books Limited
239 Kensington High Street, London W8 6SA

This edition first produced in 1998 for The Book People
Hall Wood Avenue, Haydock, St Helens WA11 9UL

ISBN 1 85613 459 8

3 5 7 9 10 8 6 4

Printed in Hong Kong